Dear Parent:

Your child's love of reading s

Every child learns to read in a different way and at his or her own speed. Some go back and forth between reading levels and read favorite books again and again. Others read through each level in order. You can help your young reader improve and become more confident by encouraging his or her own interests and abilities. From books your child reads with you to the first books he or she reads alone, there are I Can Read Books for every stage of reading:

SHARED READING
Basic language, word repetition, and whimsical illustrations, ideal for sharing with your emergent reader

BEGINNING READING
Short sentences, familiar words, and simple concepts for children eager to read on their own

READING WITH HELP
Engaging stories, longer sentences, and language play for developing readers

READING ALONE
Complex plots, challenging vocabulary, and high-interest topics for the independent reader

I Can Read Books have introduced children to the joy of reading since 1957. Featuring award-winning authors and illustrators and a fabulous cast of beloved characters, I Can Read Books set the standard for beginning readers.

A lifetime of discovery begins with the magical words "I Can Read!"

*Visit www.icanread.com for information
on enriching your child's reading experience.*

I Can Read® and I Can Read Book® are trademarks of HarperCollins Publishers.

Copyright © 2020 DC Comics & WBEI.
WONDER WOMAN 1984 and all related characters and elements © & ™ DC Comics and Warner Bros.
Entertainment Inc.
WB SHIELD: ™ & © WBEI. (S20)

Library of Congress Control Number: 2019957882
ISBN 978-0-06-296338-3

Typography by Erica De Chavez

20 21 22 23 24   LSCC   10 9 8 7 6 5 4 3 2 1   ❖   First Edition

WW84
WONDER · WOMAN
DC

MEET
WONDER
WOMAN

Adapted by
Alexandra West

Wonder Woman created
by William Moulton Marston

Screenplay by:
Patty Jenkins
Geoff Johns
Dave Callaham

Story by:
Patty Jenkins
Geoff Johns

HARPER
An Imprint of HarperCollinsPublishers

This is Diana Prince.

She may look normal,

but Diana has a secret.

She is actually a Super Hero
named Wonder Woman!
She does a lot of saving the world.
Diana keeps her identity secret
to protect those close to her from villains.

Wonder Woman has special abilities.
She can run faster and jump higher
than a normal human.
She is also very strong.
Her powers come in handy
when she needs to save someone.

Wonder Woman protects
the innocent.
Whether you are young or old,
she will protect you from danger.

Diana was not always a Super Hero.

She was once a little girl

living among other warriors.

Diana was the most determined.

She was also the most stubborn.

Diana was fast and strong, but she
would face challenges.
She would make mistakes before she could
become the hero we know today.

Through the years, Diana learned
many important lessons.
She became a powerful hero
who never forgot the importance of truth.

Diana wears her golden armor
whenever she needs extra protection
to save the world.
The golden armor is made
to look like an eagle.

When Diana isn't being a Super Hero,
she has a normal job.
Diana works at a museum
full of ancient objects.
She loves working at the museum.

Diana is a gifted historian.

She studies ancient artifacts.

Diana has been alive a long time
and has seen many things.

Diana is immortal.

Immortal means that Diana

can live forever.

Diana has lived for many years.

She still looks like a young woman.

Diana has not changed,
but the world around her has.
Everything is bright and colorful.
The world now has fancy televisions.

Diana is living far from her home.

It's hard for her to make friends.

Then Diana meets Dr. Barbara Minerva.

Barbara is clumsy.
She bumps into Diana,
scattering all her papers.
Diana helps her new friend
pick up the papers.

Diana gets to know Barbara over lunch.

She realizes that Barbara

is a special person.

Barbara is very smart,

but she doesn't believe in herself.

Barbara does not have confidence.

Diana decides to help Barbara.

Diana thinks that their friendship

will help Barbara see

that she is special.

But Barbara doesn't like who she is.

She tries to be someone she is not.

Instead of being kind and gentle,

Barbara is overcome with a mystical power.

Soon Barbara becomes evil.

She becomes The Cheetah!

Wonder Woman needs to stop The Cheetah.
But Wonder Woman learns there
are more villains than she thinks.

Maxwell Lord is a businessman
who wants to be rich and powerful.
Maxwell will stop anyone who gets in his way.

With two major threats to the planet,
Wonder Woman will need some help.
Thankfully, Steve Trevor is back.

Diana thought she had lost Steve
over sixty years ago.
But one day Steve magically returns!
Steve is ready to help Diana.
They will tackle the threats together.

Despite these threats,

Diana uses her powers for good.

She is strong and brave.

Diana is Wonder Woman!

Turn the page for more on this moment from the film!

Welcome to
⇔ 1984 ⇔

Need the latest leg warmers? Or maybe you want to try that new hot-dog-on-a-stick place? Tweens and teens are at the mall . . . and so is Wonder Woman.

Then maybe after you've picked out some new workout clothes, you could check out the hottest fashions today!

Once you're done, you're going to want to relax with
a state-of-the-art TV set. But don't touch that dial.
Maxwell Lord is on!

Arch FRENEMY

Dr. Barbara Minerva is nervous for her first day at the Smithsonian Museum.

Then a mysterious change takes over Barbara. She feels like she can conquer the world in her new dress and high heels.

Barbara quickly realizes that this change has also made her very powerful. Almost mighty.

When Barbara's power grows too strong, only Wonder Woman can put a stop to it. Even if that means taking on her friend, now known as The Cheetah!

A NEW
THREAT

While Wonder Woman battles The Cheetah,
another evil force looms over the city. Maxwell
Lord is bent on gaining power and won't let
anything stand in his way. Will Wonder Woman
be able to take on Maxwell and save her friend?